The Not-So-Scary Dog

By
Alanna Propst, MD

Illustrated by
Michelle Simpson

MAGINATION PRESS • Washington, DC • American Psychological Association

Dedicated to my family.
Special thanks to Dr. Chandra Magill for her support and guidance during this process—AP

Copyright © 2021 by Alanna Propst. Illustrations copyright © 2021 by Michelle Simpson. Published in 2021 by Magination Press, an imprint of the American Psychological Association. All rights reserved. Except as permitted under the United States Copyright Act of 1976, no part of this publication may be reproduced or distributed in any form or by any means, or stored in a database or retrieval system, without the prior written permission of the publisher.

Magination Press is a registered trademark of the American Psychological Association. Order books at maginationpress.org or call 1-800-374-2721.

Book design by Rachel Ross

Printed by Sonic Media Solutions, Inc., Medford, NY

Library of Congress Cataloging-in-Publication Data
Names: Propst, Alanna, author. | Simpson, Michelle (Illustrator), illustrator.
Title: The not-so-scary dog / by Alanna Propst, MD ; illustrated by Michelle Simpson.
Description: Washington, DC: Magination Press, [2021] | "American Psychological Association." | Summary: A young boy and his mother hatch a step-by-step plan to overcome his fear of dogs. Includes a note to parents and caregivers about anxiety, anxiety disorders, and exposure therapy.
Identifiers: LCCN 2019056326 | ISBN 9781433832048 (hardcover)
Subjects: CYAC: Stories in rhyme. | Fear—Fiction. | Anxiety—Fiction. | Exposure therapy—Fiction. | Dogs—Fiction.
Classification: LCC PZ8.3.P936547 No 2021 | DDC [E]—dc23
LC record available at https://lccn.loc.gov/2019056326

Manufactured in the United States of America
10 9 8 7 6 5 4 3 2 1

"Oh Tommy, you've got mail, it's from Joey down the street.
An invite to his birthday bash, it sounds like such a treat!
A trampoline and games, and even prizes to be won.
Then pizza? Cake? An ice-cream truck? Oh wow, this sounds so fun!"

"He's eight feet tall and barks a lot;
he slobbers and is hairy.
Oh please don't make me go to this,
the dog is way too scary!

His teeth are long and sharp like swords; he doesn't look too kind. I think I'll just stay home that day, or else I'll lose my mind!"

"You know, I get just how you feel! I used to fear dogs too.
But then I tried exposure, a technique I'll now teach you.
Exposure means to not avoid the things that cause alarm,
Since getting close is the best way to learn they won't cause harm."

"Oh no," I said, "be near a dog? This makes me really scared.
I do not like this plan at all. I feel so unprepared."
"Of course," Mom said. "We'll choose small steps
and take it nice and slow,
since if we pick a task too hard, you're likely to say no."

Mom went online for pictures of a puppy in a yard.
It made me slightly anxious, but I thought, "That's not so hard."
We looked at dogs both big and small until I wasn't frightened.
My breathing slowed, my shaking stopped,
my chest no longer tightened.

To my surprise, one made me smile—I even found him cute:
A curly golden puppy dog who chewed a rubber boot!
Another made me chuckle 'cause his fur looked just like cotton,
and after several minutes more, my fear was near forgotten.

The next day we watched videos that Mom found on her phone.
The first was of a mountain dog who munched a big white bone.

The next was of a dog who bounced a ball up on his nose.
Another showed a puppy wet from chewing on a hose.

My favorite showed a big dog that was playing with a bunny,
I laughed and said to Mom, "Who knew that dogs could be so funny?"

To watch these scenes, it did feel hard, but only when beginning,
and as I felt my fear go down, I couldn't keep from grinning.

The next goal was my idea, Mom took me when I asked.
We visited a farm to watch the dogs run in the grass.

My fear was high when we arrived, my heart began to speed.
I wanted to just run but that is not what we'd agreed.

I focused on the cutest pup, ears floppy and eyes brown.
And as his curly tail did wag, my heart just settled down.

I was still scared but must admit the puppies had some charm.
We waited till my worry passed before we left the farm.

The next day Mom and I went out to go play in the park, and as I walked up to the swings, I heard a close, loud bark.

I looked around and saw a dog and noted that my fear was pretty low considering the dog was very near.

The dog was brown with four huge paws,
and lots of frizzy hair.
"Oh my," I heard my mother say,
"he's huge, just like a bear."

Before, this would have gotten me to turn and run away,
but now I made the braver choice: to stay right there and play.

I soared up on the swings so high and still was on my guard,
but after several minutes, thought again, "This isn't hard."
I felt so brave and very strong, just like a superhero.
I climbed and ran and laughed until my fear had gone to zero.

I wandered closer to the dog and played a minute longer.

As the seconds ticked on by, I felt myself get stronger. I gathered all my courage and decided to go ask to gently touch the giant dog and so complete my task.

I pet his fur and scratched his ears (his owner said I could),
my worry faded yet again, just like Mom said it would.

We played a few quick games of fetch.
My fear just disappeared!
I told my mom, she hugged me, and we
laughed and jumped and cheered.

I laughed and played and joked
at the best party of the year.
To think I almost missed it all,
and just because of fear.

I'd like to overcome my fear
but really have my doubts."
"Oh Mary," I said with a grin,
"we've lots to talk about."

Reader's Note

Anxiety is the fear, worry, or discomfort we experience when faced with an object or situation that we think is harmful. In many cases, anxiety is both normal and necessary. In fact, it is in part what has allowed the human race to survive thus far! Anxiety kept our ancestors vigilant while hunting for food, so as not to be eaten by a lion. It is what keeps us aware when we are crossing a busy street. Anxiety becomes a problem if it begins to interfere with the way that we act or feel on a daily basis. When this happens, regular anxiety has become an anxiety disorder.

Without treatment, anxiety disorders can become extremely disruptive to daily life. A child or teenager with anxiety may start to do poorly in school, stop spending time with friends, or become depressed, and these issues can have lasting consequences. The good news is that anxiety disorders are very treatable. While this book tells the story of how Tommy uses exposure therapy to overcome his phobia, which is one type of anxiety disorder, exposure therapy can be helpful for many types of anxieties.

Exposure therapy is a form of cognitive behavioral therapy in which one is exposed to something that triggers anxiety. When we avoid an object or situation that causes anxiety, we learn that we stayed safe because we stayed away. Instead, we need to learn that we can be close to whatever we are scared of and still be safe. Being near something we are afraid of can be unpleasant and uncomfortable, so exposure therapy often occurs in small steps, getting a little bit closer to the feared object or situation with each task. This may seem as though exposure therapy gets harder as it progresses, but this is not the case: each step is done until the anxiety is gone or minimal, and serves as practice so that the next steps do not actually feel as difficult as it would have felt before therapy. With each step, we learn that we are still safe despite having been close to the feared object or situation. Parents can help their children through this process in several ways:

Share your own experiences with anxiety. Children suffering from anxiety may feel alone or ashamed about what they are going through. If you talk about your own experiences, your child can see that they are not strange or different. Knowing that you have dealt with anxiety can also help your child feel that you understand their experience. If you have been able to overcome your anxiety, talking about your story can show your child that fears can indeed be conquered.

Pause throughout the book to explain how exposure works by using examples from the story. The main idea to convey is the difference between avoidance and exposure. Avoidance teaches our brains that we are safe only because we stayed out of harm's way. Exposure lets us see that what we are scared of is not actually dangerous. For example, as Tommy looks at the pictures of dogs in his first task, he is slowly able to see that he is not in danger and he calms down with each photo until he isn't afraid. You can also point out that Tommy's tasks may appear more difficult as the book progresses, but that Tommy does not experience them this way. He becomes more and more comfortable as he observes photos, then videos, then dogs running in a field, and finally a dog in the park—first far away and then up close. It can help to draw a parallel to something your child has learned how to do that got easier with practice and ultimately increased in complexity. For example, learning how to ride a bike and then taking off the training wheels. You can break down how your child accomplished that task, highlighting the fact that each part got easier with time, and that they were then able to go to the next step.

Stop throughout the book and ask your child questions. Children learn best when they are engaged and actively participating. Here are a few suggestions:

- **Throughout the book, ask, "What do you think Tommy is feeling?"**

- **When Tommy describes the dog as eight feet tall with teeth like swords, ask, "Do you think this sounds realistic?"**

- **After Tommy completes the first few tasks, ask, "Why do you think his anxiety is going down?"**

- **"What does it mean when Tommy says the dog had been bigger in his head?"**

- **"What do you think Tommy and Mary have to talk about?"**

- **"What have you learned from this book?"**

Plan your own list of tasks to conquer your child's fear. These should appear to increase in difficulty; this is also known as a hierarchy. You can start by having your child name the thing that frightens them the most related to their fear—something they would rate as a 10/10 on a fear scale. Then have them name something related to their fear that frightens them much less, that they think they can accomplish with minimal distress—something they would rate as a 1 or 2/10.

Once these benchmarks are established, they can then fill in the steps in between. Once you've come up with the steps, you can start to tackle them! An important aspect of completing a hierarchy is repeating each individual step until it causes minimal to no anxiety. This allows your child to gain practice and confidence so that the next step does not seem so hard. And just as Tommy's mother does, don't forget to act as your child's cheerleader—hugs, laughter, praise, and rewards go a long way!

Be present to support and encourage your child. Parental involvement in exposure therapy is extremely important. Exposure techniques can be stressful! First, Tommy describes high levels of anxiety as his mother explains the notion of exposure therapy to him. This type of anxiety is called "anticipatory anxiety," since it occurs when someone is anticipating, or waiting for, something to happen. And of course Tommy has some anxiety at the start of each new task! By supporting, encouraging, and being by your child's side throughout exposure techniques, you can decrease their stress level—and make it more likely that they will stick with their tasks and succeed!

Sometimes, in order to decrease their child's anxiety, parents will help their child avoid the object of their fear. While this is done with the best of intentions, it is not particularly helpful and in fact will cause the anxiety to continue. Therefore, another way to help your child is to stop helping them avoid the thing that scares them.

If your child's daily life is being affected by their anxiety, they may benefit from professional help. Do not hesitate to ask your child's primary care physician for guidance and for a referral if needed.

Alanna J. Propst is a psychiatrist who graduated from McGill University in both the Psychiatry Residency Program as well as the Child and Adolescent Psychiatry Subspecialty Residency Program, and has worked in inpatient, outpatient, and emergency room settings. This is her debut picture book. Alanna lives in Montreal, Canada.

Michelle Simpson is a professional illustrator and designer. She graduated with a BAA in illustration from Sheridan College. Michelle is the recipient of the Brenda Clark Book Award and the Cheltenham Illustration Award. She lives in the Niagara Region in Canada.

Visit michellescribbles.com and michiscribbles.etsy.com
@Michiscribbles
@MichelleScribbles

Magination Press is the children's book imprint of the American Psychological Association. Through APA's publications, the association shares with the world mental health expertise and psychological knowledge. Magination Press books reach young readers and their parents and caregivers to make navigating life's challenges a little easier. It's the combined power of psychology and literature that makes a Magination Press book special.

Visit maginationpress.org
@MaginationPress